MY STRONG MIND

A STORY ABOUT DEVELOPING MENTAL STRENGTH
by NIELS VAN HOVE

For my Three Beautiful Girls Poppy, Coco and Missy.

Published in Australia by Truebridges Media
Email: info@mentaltoughness.online
Website: www.mentaltoughness.online

First published in Australia 2017
Copyright© Niels van Hove 2017

National Library of Australia Cataloguing-in-Publication entry
Creator: Van Hove, Niels
Title: My Strong Mind
ISBN: 978-0-6480859-1-1
Target Audience: For primary school age
Subjects: Juvenile fiction. Confidence in children. Self-esteem. Toughness (personal trait).

Cover layout and illustrations by Diki (graphic designer)
Typesetting by Nelly Murariu (PixBeeDesign.com)
Printed by Createspace

Disclaimer
All care has been taken in the preparation of the information herein, but no responsibility can be accepted by the publisher or author for any damages resulting from the misinterpretation of this work. All contact details given in this book were current at the time of publication, but are subject to change.

Kate is a sporty and happy girl.
She does well at school and has many friends.
But like every girl, she faces difficult
situations at home or at school. Sometimes
things just don't go as she likes.

She is slow to get ready for school,

making her parents grumpy with her.

All her friends can do **Cartwheels,** but she cannot.

She is afraid to stand In front of the class

to do **show and tell.**

Her friends sometimes say mean things.

One day, Kate read a book about strong minds. She learned that everyone has their own brain and can make up their own mind. You can teach your mind what to do so it can **tackle** any challenge with a positive attitude.

When you practice, your mind gets smarter and stronger.
It is OK to try and fail. Because
over time your mind can help you
get better at anything you want.
Kate decided to use her mind
with all her **challenges.**

That evening Kate wrote a list of all her tasks she had
to do in the morning. Get dressed, brush hair, brush teeth,
pack school bag, and many more things.
The next morning, she told her mind, do one task
at a time until the whole list is done.

Kate focussed her mind on her task list.
One by one she finished the tasks,
and **ticked** them off the list
as she worked through.
She was ready for school
with plenty of **time.**

Her parents were very surprised.

When Kate arrived at school her friends were doing cartwheels. Kate never joined in because she couldn't do a cartwheel, and she did not want to fail in front of her friends. Kate told her mind, **it's ok to try and fail.** Because every time I try, I get a little bit better.

She tried her hardest,
throwing her hands onto the ground and lifting
her legs, and she almost got the cartwheel right.
Her friends giggled, but
Kate felt good that she had practiced.
She told her mind, *well done.*

That day it was her turn to do show and tell in front of the whole class. Standing before a big group always made Kate very nervous. She told her mind, *it is OK to feel a bit scared, you can do this.*

Kate closed her eyes and imagined how she would deliver a great **show and tell,** speaking clearly, making eye contact and smiling more. Because she practiced in her mind, she wasn't so nervous in front of the class, and even enjoyed her show and tell.

During lunch she sat around with her friends in the schoolyard. Some of her friends started to be **mean** to her. Kate got very angry and felt like **screaming.** Then Kate told her mind, *count to ten.*

5 6 7 8 9 10

That helped her calm down so
she didn't feel like screaming anymore.
Kate told her friends in a
calm voice that she didn't want
to be treated like that
then walked off.

In the evening Kate had a **basketball** game.
Her team was very unlucky that night.
They were missing some of their best
players and hardly any ball went
in to the **hoop.** The other team
had many strong players and
they were way ahead
in the score.

Kate was tired and felt like giving up.
Then she told her mind, *keep trying your best.*
Kate kept running and running as long as she could.
Her team lost the game but Kate still felt proud
that she did the best she could.

Kate was very tired from a long day but couldn't sleep. She kept thinking about all the things that happened that day. Kate got out of bed and found her dad lying on the couch **watching** television while glancing at his phone.

'Daddy,' Kate said.

Her dad wasn't really listening.

'Daddy,'

Kate said more loudly. 'You are not listening to what I say.'

Her dad looked up at her.

'Did you know you can tell your mind to
stop looking at your phone and listen to me?'

'You are right,' said her dad. 'I'll put my phone away
and **concentrate** on you.'
'Can't you sleep?'

Kate shook her head.
'Let's play a game to relax called rock the boat.'

Kate and her dad both lay down on their backs
and put a little paper boat on their tummy.

They listened to some quiet music and
took deep breaths.

Breathe in
1, 2, 3, 4...

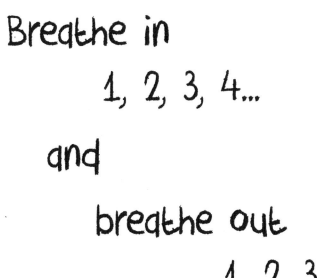

and

breathe out
1, 2, 3, 4...

Breathing made the boat rock on their tummies.

After a couple of minutes,
Kate's mind calmed and she started to feel sleepy.

Her dad carried Kate to bed and tucked her in.
Kate asked, 'What were your three favourite things
of the day, Daddy?'

It made Kate feel good when she heard all the positive things her dad had to say about his day. 'Well, watching you do your best at basketball was surely one of my **favourite** things of the day,' said her dad. This made Kate feel happy.

Kate fell asleep to her dad telling all his favourite things,

and her mind grew just a little

bit stronger that day.

NOTES FOR PARENTS

What is Mental Toughness?

Mental Toughness* is a combination of resilience, curiosity and drive to grow yourself and confidence in your own abilities and interactions with people. Mental Toughness has been used in elite sport psychology for many years to increase performance and it applies to everyday life too.

There are four attributes that characterise Mental Toughness, also called The Four Cs:

➤ **Commitment:** I promise to do it. I will set a goal and do whatever it takes to deliver.

➤ **Control**: I really believe I can do it. I will keep my emotions in check when doing it.

➤ **Challenge:** I'm driven to do it, I will take a chance and acceptable risk. Setbacks will make me stronger.

➤ **Confidence:** I believe I have the ability to do it. I can stand my ground if I need to.

Studies in the occupational, educational, and sports worlds consistently show that Mental Toughness is directly related to wellbeing, aspirations, employability, and performance. Furthermore, men and women are equally mentally tough. Mental Toughness is a plastic personality trait and can be developed or improved.

Like us, we can be sure our children will have to deal with adversity, stress, and challenges during their life. The examples in this book show real-life challenges from my 7 and 9-year-old daughters, and give examples of how small interventions can lead to better outcomes.

These are goals setting, positive self-talk, accept failure as learning, visualisation of a problem, breathing or mindfulness exercises, gratitude, and controlled distraction. The exercise 'rock the boat' is available on the free mindfulness app Smiling Mind.

Try it, we use it at home with the family.

As an introduction for parents to Mental Toughness and many more intervention techniques, I suggest my e-book Building Mental Toughness: Practical help to be yourself at your best. This book is available on my website **www.mentaltoughness.online.**

About the author

Niels is the founding coach at **www.mentaltoughness.online.** He became an accredited Mental Toughness coach following a rough period in his career and now helps people to get the best out of themselves. He is passionate to educate the world about Mental Toughness and he hopes this book opens a positive dialogue on the subject. He lives in Melbourne with his wife and two daughters.

* Refers to Developing Mental Toughness: Improving Performance, Wellbeing and Positive Behaviours in Others by Peter Clough and Doug Strycharczyk.

www.mentaltoughness.online